Resurrection Bridge

Adrian B. Verano

Ukiyoto Publishing

All global publishing rights are held by
Ukiyoto Publishing

Published in 2023

Content Copyright © Adrian B. Verano

ISBN 9789358466560

All rights reserved.
No part of this publication may be reproduced, transmitted, or stored in a retrieval system, in any form by any means, electronic, mechanical, photocopying, recording or otherwise, without the prior permission of the publisher.

The moral rights of the author have been asserted.

This is a work of fiction. Names, characters, businesses, places, events, locales, and incidents are either the products of the author's imagination or used in a fictitious manner. Any resemblance to actual persons, living or dead, or actual events is purely coincidental.

This book is sold subject to the condition that it shall not by way of trade or otherwise, be lent, resold, hired out or otherwise circulated, without the publisher's prior consent, in any form of binding or cover other than that in which it is published.
www.ukiyoto.com

The car swerved on the road as a motorcycle approached them from the opposite direction.

The car safely maneuvered to the side of the road, narrowly avoiding a collision with the motorcycle.

The place where they came to a halt, the place where their journey converged, was none other than the Resurrection Bridge—a site haunted by Yuri's deepest regrets. It was here that the greatest sorrow of her life unfolded, a mistake for which she sought redemption and forgiveness from the divine.

FLASHBACK

A few years back, YURI found herself facing a critical decision. In the midst of grappling with the complexities of life, she had to navigate the challenging path of abortion. It was on that very Bridge, Yuri fell from years ago and had to udergo abortion hence.

"Oh No! She seems to be falling down."

Paul was Yuri's jobless boyfriend at the time. It was an accident, a consequence of impulsive choices fueled by the intoxicating drinks they consumed that fateful night.

Yuri was in shock and tears.

Yuri found Paul was still inside the car.

www.ingramcontent.com/pod-product-compliance
Lightning Source LLC
LaVergne TN
LVHW061628070526
838199LV00070B/6625